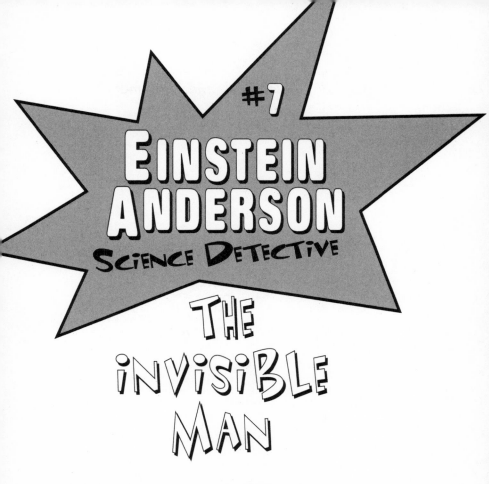

#7

EINSTEIN ANDERSON

Science Detective

THE INVISIBLE MAN

AND OTHER CASES

by Seymour Simon

illustrated by S. D. Schindler

Morrow Junior Books
NEW YORK

(Previously published as *Einstein Anderson Sees Through the Invisible Man*)

For Chloe, Joel, and Benjamin

Inquiries should be addressed to William Morrow and Company, Inc.,
1350 Avenue of the Americas, New York, NY 10019.
www. williammorrow.com
First published in 1983 by Viking Penguin
under the title *Einstein Anderson Sees Through the Invisible Man.*
Revised hardcover edition published by Morrow Junior Books in 1998.
Published by arrangement with the author.

Printed in the United States of America.

1   2   3   4   5   6   7   8   9   10

Library of Congress Cataloging-in-Publication Data
Simon, Seymour.
The invisible man and other cases/by Seymour Simon;
illustrated by S. D. Schindler.—Rev. ed.
p. cm.—(Einstein Anderson, science detective)
"First published in 1983 by Viking Penguin under the title
'Einstein Anderson sees through the invisible man'"—T. p. verso.
Summary: The sixth-grade science sleuth solves ten more puzzling cases,
one involving an allergic monster and another an invisible man.
ISBN 0-688-14447-0
[1. Science—Problems, exercises, etc.—Fiction.]   I. Schindler, S. D., ill.
II. Simon, Seymour. Einstein Anderson sees through the invisible man.
III. Title.   IV. Series: Simon, Seymour. Einstein Anderson, science detective.
PZ7.S60573In 1998   [Fic]—dc20 96-43686   CIP AC

CONTENTS

1

The Case of the

iNViSiBLE MAN

"Can anything really be invisible?" asked Mrs. Anderson, Einstein's mother. Einstein and his younger brother, Dennis, had just finished a hurried breakfast and were getting ready to catch the school bus.

"Sure," Einstein said cheerfully. "Dennis becomes invisible whenever it's his turn to wash the dishes."

"I learned that trick from you," Dennis replied, sticking out his tongue at his brother.

Mrs. Anderson smiled. She worked as a

reporter and editor on the Sparta *Tribune,* one of the town's two newspapers. Sometimes she used the things her two boys did and said in funny stories she wrote for the paper.

"I want a scientific answer, Einstein," Mrs. Anderson declared. "Not a corny joke."

Einstein pushed back his glasses, which were slipping off the end of his nose. He thought for a moment and then replied, "Lots of things are invisible. Ultraviolet rays, X rays, and many other kinds of radiation can't be seen by humans. You can't see a magnetic field or an electric current."

"Yes, yes," said Mrs. Anderson. "But can an object be invisible?"

"Well, under the right conditions glass or plastic can be invisible. Polished crystal quartz can be invisible. It all depends on just what you mean by invisible."

"What about a person?" Mrs. Anderson asked. "Could there really be an invisible man?"

"I saw a movie about the Invisible Man," Dennis said. "You couldn't see him except at the end, just when he was dying. You see, this guy—"

"I don't mean in a movie or in a book," interrupted Mrs. Anderson. "I mean for real. The chief of police has been hearing some peculiar stories about footprints that appeared by themselves and voices heard when there was no one around to make the sound. Now someone named Griffin has called a press conference for this afternoon. He says that he is able to become invisible. Do you think that's possible?"

"Probably not," replied Einstein. "But if I can go with you to the press conference and ask a few questions, I should be able to find out if it's just a hoax."

"Fine," said Mrs. Anderson. "Meet me at my office when you get out of school, and we'll go over to the conference together. And in the meantime you boys had better leave to catch the bus."

"On our way," said Einstein. "But did you hear about the invisible man who looked in the mirror to see if he still wasn't there?"

"Adam!" said Mrs. Anderson, holding her nose with one hand and pointing out the door with her other hand. "No more corny jokes this morning. You have to get to school, and I have to get to work. Out, out."

Adam was Einstein's real name. But nobody called him Adam anymore except his father and mother once in a while. Adam was twelve years old and in the sixth grade. He had been interested in science for as long as he could remember. His kindergarten teacher, Ms. Moore, had called him by the nickname of Einstein, after the most famous scientist of the twentieth century. But Einstein was not always serious. He liked jokes and puns of all kinds, the worse the better.

After school Einstein went over to the offices of the *Tribune*. Then Mrs. Anderson and Einstein drove to the local TV station, where the press conference was to take place. The conference was to be taped for showing on the local TV news that evening. There were several reporters from out of town, and the Sparta chief of police was there as well.

They must be taking this seriously, Einstein thought. But someone becoming invisible sounded like science fiction, not science fact.

"I bet Mr. Griffin's first name is Jack," Einstein whispered to his mother.

"Why, how do you know that?" Mrs. Anderson asked. She seemed surprised. "I never told you his first name. And what has his first name got to do with...?"

Just then, Diane Bergman, an anchorperson on the local TV news, came into the room. She was followed by a middle-aged man, short and thin, dressed in an old-fashioned tweed suit. They both sat down at a table in the front of the room, and Ms. Bergman spoke.

"I want to introduce Mr. Griffin. He's asked to make a short announcement and show a film he has made. Then he will answer questions."

Mr. Griffin stood up and looked around the room. "I know that some of you are skeptical about what I'm going to tell you," Mr. Griffin said. He spoke in a deep voice that sounded like an actor's. "But many people to whom I've told my story believe that I'm telling the truth. In fact, I'm writing a book about some of my adventures, and there may even be a film later on. So I'd like you to hear what I say with an open mind.

"I discovered the formula for becoming invisible among some old papers that had been in a chest my family had for many years. It seems that my great-grandfather, whom I had been named for, was the original inventor. But the formula for invisibility is dangerous. It can make a person mad. And sometimes it doesn't even work. But I have used it, and I have proof that I can become invisible. I want you to see this film. It was taken by your chief of police."

Mr. Griffin gave a signal, and the room lights darkened. A film was projected on a screen in the front. The film was badly lit and obviously had been taken by someone without much experience with a camera. The film seemed to show some objects moving without anyone moving them, and even a hat floating along in midair. The hat moved along a twisty path that led between some trees in a park that Einstein recognized.

Mr. Griffin stood up again. He pointed to the chief of police and asked, "Did you take this film, and can you tell everybody that the film was never in my possession?"

The chief of police reluctantly stood up. "I did take the film," he said. "But I can't testify to what it shows. I was so busy trying to use the camera that I'm just not sure. But I can say that the film has been under guard and that you didn't tamper with it."

"Fair enough," said Mr. Griffin. "Now are there any questions from the audience?"

"Yes," said the reporter in the front row. "Why don't you just become invisible now and prove that you can?"

"I'm afraid that I won't be able to become invisible again for months, maybe even years," said Mr. Griffin. "Otherwise, the invisibility drug will drive me crazy. I have to wait until the last little bit is out of my system."

"Excuse me, sir," said Einstein, "but I have a question."

Mr. Griffin looked amused. "Out of the mouths of babes comes truth," he said pompously. "Go right ahead, young man. I'm sure you believe me."

"I just wonder if all of you became invisible," Einstein said. "Even your eyes?"

Mr. Griffin laughed. "Every last bit became invisible," he said. "Even my eyes. Now are there any more sensible questions?"

After a few more questions the conference broke up. The reporters stood around talking to one another. Most of them seemed unsure how to write their stories.

Mrs. Anderson turned to her son. "What do you think about Mr. Griffin's story, Einstein? Do you think he really was invisible? And why did you ask that funny question about his eyes? Does that have anything to do with his story?"

"It has everything to do with his story," said Einstein. "His answer to my question and the film he showed are all the facts I need to know that the so-called Mr. Griffin couldn't possibly have been invisible."

Can you solve the mystery: How did Einstein know that Mr. Griffin was not telling the truth? (And do you know why Einstein guessed that Mr. Griffin's first name was Jack?)

Einstein smiled. "Mr. Griffin's story reminds me of the invisible mother who was upset by her invisible child. It seems he was always appearing."

"Another one of those jokes and I'll make *you* disappear," said Mrs. Anderson, trying to keep from laughing. "Tell me why you don't believe Mr. Griffin's story."

"Because if there were an invisible man, he would be blind. In order for someone to see, light rays have to be absorbed by the retina. But the retina of an invisible man would be transparent, so light rays would pass through and not be absorbed. There are other reasons as well, but that convinced me that Mr. Griffin must be lying."

"So that's why you asked him if his eyes were invisible," said Mrs. Anderson.

"Right," Einstein said. "If he were blind when he was invisible, he never would have been able to follow that twisty path through the trees. His hat certainly would have been knocked off. Griffin could have easily used black threads or thin wires to make things move in the film. The chief never would have noticed because he was so busy with the movie camera."

"But how did you know that his first name was Jack?"

"That's easy," Einstein explained. "Jack Griffin was the name that H. G. Wells used for the main character in his book *The Invisible Man*. I guessed that an invisible man who used the name Griffin would also choose the same first name Wells used for his fictional character."

"I see that Mr. Griffin is coming over this way. Do you want to speak to him?" Mrs. Anderson asked.

"Tell him that I'm sorry, but I just can't see him," Einstein replied with a grin.

2

The Case of the

Do-it-Yourself Diving Suit

"I 've tried to make my new invention as simple as possible," Stanley declared to Einstein. "I've gone wrong before because my inventions were too complicated. But my new invention is so easy to make that I'm not going to have any trouble selling thousands of them."

"I hope it works better than your automatic back scratcher," Einstein commented. "That thing ripped right through the back of my shirt. It looked as if I'd been attacked by a tiger. Mom said the shirt was too torn to be repaired. She said your back scratcher should have been named an automatic shirt destroyer."

"Every great scientist has known failure," Stanley said loftily.

"That's true, Stanley," Einstein responded with a smile. "You never make the same mistake twice with your inventions. With every invention you find a new mistake to make."

"I'll overlook that remark," Stanley said, brushing back his long black hair, which was falling into his eyes. "One day my inventions will make me famous. They may even show my originals in the Smithsonian in Washington, along with Edison's and other great inventors'."

"You think they'll be able to find the originals in this place?" Einstein asked doubtfully. He looked around the attic room that Stanley used for his inventions and experiments. The room was overflowing with all kinds of half-finished contraptions, test tubes, flasks, and other odds and ends. It looked like a mad scientist's laboratory from a horror movie. About

the only thing missing was Frankenstein's monster standing in the corner.

Stanley Roberts was in high school and a few years older than Einstein. Stanley was always inventing some new kind of gadget that he wanted to show Einstein. Einstein liked Stanley, but he also enjoyed kidding him about his mistakes in science.

"Cleaning up laboratories is not what I'm best at," Stanley admitted. "Inventing is my line. And wait till I show you what I've just finished making. With my new gadget every kid can become an explorer on his own and make discoveries in new worlds."

Einstein grinned. "Just like when the explorer Balboa discovered the Pacific Ocean and said those immortal words."

"What was that?" Stanley asked curiously.

"Long time no sea," Einstein replied.

"Ohhh!" Stanley groaned. "When will I learn not to ask you questions?"

"Well, there's one question to which I could never answer yes," Einstein said.

"What's that?" Stanley asked despite himself.

"Are you asleep?" responded Einstein.

"Stop, stop, please," Stanley moaned. "No more jokes. Just be quiet until I show you my invention."

Einstein was about to say that he was

going to keep his mouth shut because silence was golden when he caught Stanley's eye and decided not to say anything.

Stanley went over to a corner of the attic and took something off the floor. He brought it over to Einstein and held it up to show. "Look at this," he said proudly.

Einstein looked at the gadget curiously. It looked like a plastic fishbowl with a long plastic tube coming out of the bottom.

"I get it," said Einstein. "It's a training tank for goldfish who want to be explorers. Instead of just swimming around the tank, the goldfish will swim in that long tube."

"No," Stanley said contemptuously. "Though that's not a bad idea for an aquarium. Hmmm? No, forget about it. This may look like a fishbowl, but it's actually an underwater helmet when you hold it upside down. The tube is the air hose that goes to the surface."

"Are you kidding?" asked Einstein. "The diving helmet using an air pump was invented by Augustus Siebe in 1819, more than a hundred and fifty years ago. You didn't invent anything new at all."

"Maybe not," Stanley admitted. "But my invention is much cheaper and easier to use. I don't use an air pump at all. The tube just goes to the surface and is attached to a float so that it stays above the water. All the diver has to do is breathe the air through the tube. The helmet costs so little to make that I can sell it for just a few dollars and still make a profit. I'll be rich and famous overnight."

"That night is liable to be a dark horse," said Einstein. "That's what I call a nightmare," he explained. "Sorry about the joke, Stanley, but your invention is useless."

Can you solve the mystery: How did Einstein know that Stanley's diving helmet would not work?

"I don't understand how you can say that, Einstein," Stanley complained. "Diving suits work. Scuba apparatus works. Why won't my diving helmet work?"

"It's a matter of water pressure," Einstein explained. "For every foot you dive beneath the surface, the pressure of water increases more than sixty-two pounds per square foot. Ten feet down, the water pressure is six hundred and twenty-five pounds per square foot. The water pressure on your chest makes breathing through a tube impossible for any length of time. The deepest you can go and still take a hard breath is two or three feet."

"That still doesn't explain why diving suits and scubas work," said Stanley.

"They both provide air under pressure," Einstein said. "The pressure of the air from a surface pump or in compressed-air tanks allows your lungs to expand against the water pressure."

"The water pressure on a deep-sea diver must be really tremendous," said Stanley.

"Right," agreed Einstein. "Even a submarine would crack like an eggshell if it went too far down. Only a specially constructed deep-diving ship like the bathyscaphe can dive down to the depths of the ocean without being crushed."

"It must be frightening to be so far down with all that water pressing all around," said Stanley.

"Well, you know what they call a frightened deep-sea swimmer?" asked Einstein.

"What?" asked Stanley.

"A yellow submarine," replied Einstein.

3

The Case of the

MISSING
PITCH

It was a beautiful Saturday in September. Almost everyone in Einstein's sixth-grade class was playing in a softball game at the school ball field. Einstein was pitching for one side, and his best friend, Margaret, was pitching for the other side. The score was 18–13, with Einstein's side leading.

"This is a real pitcher's duel," Einstein said to Mike, the shortstop on his team. "Nobody has scored a hundred runs yet."

"Maybe that's because it's only the second

inning," Mike observed. "And I've only been up to bat eleven times."

"I knew there was some reason for the low score," Einstein said, laughing. "The game's taking so long, I forgot what inning it is."

Einstein walked to the mound and checked his team. Everyone was in position. He pitched a high, soft floater. The batter swung and hit a pop fly that fell for a double. Einstein called a time-out and gestured his infield in for a conference at the mound.

"What do you want, Einstein?" asked Sally, who played first base. "You want to try out some new strategy? Like striking out someone?"

"I never heard of someone striking out in our softball games," Einstein said. "What I wanted to tell you was why Cinderella was such a poor baseball player. You see, she always ran away from the ball."

Everyone groaned. "With jokes like that, you deserve to lose," Mike said.

"We better not cry if we lose," Einstein responded. "Because then we'd be called a *bawl* club. B-A-W-L. Get it?"

"Ugh," said Sally. "I got it, and I hope it's not catching."

"Let's play ball, Einstein," said Mike as he walked back to his position.

"Sure," said Einstein. "As the waiter said when someone ordered pancakes, batter up!"

Everyone went back to his or her position. Einstein was about to make the next pitch when Pat and Herman trotted over to the field. Pat Burns was the kind of kid that thinks every mean trick is funny—as long as it happens to someone else.

Pat's nickname was Pat the Brat, but nobody called him that to his face. He was too big and too mean. Pat's only friend was Herman. Herman was almost as big and mean as Pat.

Pat walked onto the field and looked around. "Would you believe that, Herman?" he said. "Look who's trying to play ball!"

"It's Einstein and Mike, and there's Sally, and..." Herman started to name the players.

"I know, I know," Pat said impatiently. "You're not exactly dumb, Herman, but it took you ten years to learn how to wave bye-bye."

"Are we going somewhere, Pat?" Herman asked.

"Forget it," Pat said. He turned to Einstein. "How come you didn't ask me to play ball with you, Mr. Four-Eyed Einstein Anderson? Afraid I'd beat you?"

Einstein was not afraid of standing up to Pat and Herman, but he usually tried to handle them by outthinking them. "If you want to play, we'll put you and Herman on a team. If you don't want to play ball, then get off the field."

Pat laughed derisively. "Play ball with you!" he declared. "Not me! I can catch a ball better than you with one eye closed."

"That's not very likely," Einstein said mildly.

"Want to bet?" asked Pat. "I bet you your baseball glove that I can catch a ball better with one eye closed than you can with both your eyes open."

"O.K.," said Einstein. "I'll make that bet. But what do I get if you lose?"

"Not a chance," Pat boasted. "And we can talk about that if I lose. Which will never

25

happen. I can catch a ball better than
anybody in the class. I'll be happy to win your
mitt," he concluded, pointing to Einstein's
baseball glove.

The rules for the contest were set up. Pat would throw five balls to Einstein, and Einstein would throw the same to Pat. Pat had to wear a blindfold over one eye. The one who caught the most balls would be the winner.

Margaret was very upset. "Are you sure you know what you're doing, Einstein?" she asked in a whisper. "Pat really *can* catch better than you. And he can throw the ball higher, too. You may wind up losing your mitt to him."

"Trust me...and science," Einstein said. "Pat is not going to win this contest."

Can you solve the mystery: Why was Einstein so confident that he would catch the ball better than Pat?

The contest didn't take long. Einstein caught four out of the five balls that Pat threw at him. Pat caught only one of the balls that Einstein threw. Twice Pat nearly got hit in the face with the ball.

By the end of the contest Pat was furious. "I don't understand why I couldn't catch the ball," he fumed. "It never seemed to be in the right place. Did you put something on the ball, Einstein?"

"No," Einstein responded. "How could I? We were both using the same ball. And by the way, now that you've lost the bet, what are you going to give me?"

"Herman can carry your books around school for the next few days," Pat said with a mean smile. "Come on, Herman. Let's leave these cheaters."

"Pat has a great sense of humor," Einstein observed as Pat and Herman walked off. "You can easily amuse him by slipping on a banana peel and breaking your leg."

"Never mind about that," said Margaret. "Just tell me how you made Pat miss catching the balls you threw."

"I didn't make him miss. It was trying to catch with one eye that did it. You see, each of your eyes sees an object from a slightly different angle. That helps you to tell how far away an object is. You can judge where an object is much better when you use two eyes. Pat just couldn't tell where the ball was, so he kept on missing it."

"Pat's such a show-off," Sally said. "He never should have made that bet."

"Right," Einstein agreed. "Pat is the kind of show-off that's always shown up in a showdown."

4
The Case of the
ALLERGIC MONSTER

I've got the perfect title for our science-fiction play, Einstein," Margaret said. "*The Case of the Allergic Monster.* How does that sound?"

"That's a real catchy title," Einstein admitted. "Which reminds me. Did you know what brings monster babies? Frankenstork."

Margaret giggled. "Einstein!" she said warningly. "We don't have time for your silly jokes. We have to write this play and bring it to class next week."

"Right," agreed Einstein. "But I know you'll be happy to hear that monsters bring presents to their mothers on Mummy's Day."

"Is that so," Margaret said. She thought for a minute. "I suppose you know what to say when you meet a two-headed monster?"

"Hello, hello," said Einstein.

"O.K., I give up." Margaret laughed. "You know more bad jokes than I do. But I still think I know more science than you do."

Margaret Michaels was Einstein's classmate and friend. She was also his rival for the title of best science student in Sparta Middle School. Margaret and Einstein often did science experiments together and talked about important things like black holes in space, laser beams, animal behavior, and who was the better scientist and baseball player.

"I'll call it a draw if you make us some peanut butter and jelly sandwiches," Einstein said, smiling agreeably.

"You're always hungry, Einstein." Margaret sighed. "I'll make the sandwiches, and you can make some hot cocoa. We can go over the plot of our play while we're eating."

"Right," said Einstein. "I just don't like working on an empty stomach."

As Margaret and Einstein were preparing the food in the kitchen, Nova wandered in. Nova was Margaret's dog, a black-and-white springer spaniel. Nova was always begging for table scraps. She liked any kind of "people food." Einstein fed her bits of bread when Margaret wasn't looking.

"If you've finished feeding Nova," Margaret said without turning around, "I'd like to eat these sandwiches and get on with our work."

Margaret brought the sandwiches over to the kitchen table. "Let me summarize the plot of our play," she said. "Two astronauts are circling Earth in Space Station Number One. The space station is in a condition of weightlessness so that construction is easier. The first scene will show Bernice and Joan at work on a space radio."

"Couldn't we name the astronauts Bernice and Tom?" Einstein objected mildly. "You're using female names for both astronauts."

"I just wanted to make the point that women can be just as much at home in space as men," explained Margaret. "But maybe it *would* be better if we have equality, so one of the astronauts can be named Tom.

"Anyway, the astronauts start to hear something peculiar coming over their radio," Margaret continued. "There are some scary sounds, and all of a sudden there's a big thump."

"The aliens have landed," Einstein said. "Let's have the aliens disable the electrical system in the space station so that the lights will go out. The play will be much more frightening if the scene is dark."

"I don't think we can do that," said Margaret. "We need to have the electricity working so that the monsters can be killed in the end."

"I thought the monsters were allergic to hot water," Einstein said. "And one of the astronauts will accidentally spill the hot water on a monster to kill it just when it looks like

the situation is hopeless. The monster will shrivel away just like the wicked witch did in the movie *The Wizard of Oz*."

"That's just it," explained Margaret. "I was going to have an astronaut making a pot of hot tea over an electric stove. When the monster comes through the door unexpectedly, the astronaut will throw the pot at it. The hot water from the pot will drench the monster, and the monster will dissolve. To the monster who comes from a dry planet, the hot water will be like a superacid."

Einstein pushed his glasses back. "I don't think we can do that," he objected. "It's scientifically wrong."

"This is science fiction," Margaret said. "We can imagine the monster any way we want."

"It's not the monster," Einstein said. "It's the hot water that's not scientific."

Can you solve the mystery: What is wrong with the hot water in Margaret's story?

"How can hot water be unscientific?" Margaret asked crossly. "It's just ordinary hot water heated up in a teapot."

"That's the problem," said Einstein. "It's heating the water in a teapot that won't work under a weightless condition in space. Even after an hour the water at the top of the teapot would still be cold."

"But I told you that the electricity would stay on in the space station. So the electric hot plate will be working. The teapot can be secured in place over the hot plate so it won't drift away. I don't see why the water won't get hot."

"Because water on Earth heats mostly by convection," Einstein explained. "The water at the bottom of a teapot on Earth is heated and becomes lighter. The cold, heavier water at the top sinks down, gets heated, and rises again. That's called a convection current. But there are no convection currents in a weightless condition in a space station because nothing is lighter or heavier than anything else."

"So the water at the top of the teapot won't get hot at all," said Margaret slowly.

"It will after a number of hours," said Einstein. "But that means that no astronaut would use a teapot and a hot plate to make hot water. It would be much easier to use microwaves to heat water."

"Well, then that's solved," Margaret declared. "We'll just have Bernice using microwaves to boil hot water."

"You'd better not have Bernice pour the hot water down a rabbit hole," Einstein commented with a smile, "unless you want a hot, cross bunny."

5

The Case of the

UNBREAKABLE STRING

Einstein was in the school yard during lunchtime. He was having a catch with his friends Mike and Barney when he saw Pat Burns coming over. Pat looked worried.

"I wonder where Pat's sidekick is," Einstein said in a low voice. "You usually don't see Pat without Herman."

"Maybe Herman got lost walking out of the lunchroom," Barney commented. "After all, today is Monday, and Herman might need retraining after being away for the weekend."

"Did you ever see Pat look so worried?" Mike asked. "You'd think the strongest and meanest kid in the sixth grade would have nothing to worry about."

"Well, we're sure to find out," said Einstein. "Pat's headed straight for us."

"Hiya, everybody," Pat said with a strained smile as he came up to the group. "I hope you're having a nice catch," he added.

"Huh?!" exclaimed Einstein, Mike, and Barney. They all stared at Pat incredulously. They could not remember the last time Pat had been so polite.

Pat didn't seem to notice. "Could I talk to you for a second, Einstein?" he asked nervously.

"You are talking to me, Pat," Einstein said.

"I mean privately," Pat said. "Mike and Barney can go somewhere else to have a catch." Pat glared at them.

Einstein looked at his friends. "Don't bother moving," he said. "Pat and I will just take a walk. I'll be back in a minute.

"Well, what is it, Pat?" Einstein asked as they walked to a quiet part of the school yard.

"You look like a nervous clock," he added with a smile. "All wound up."

"Ha, ha." Pat laughed weakly. "You're always joking, Einstein. But this is no joke. I'm in trouble with Tiger Martin. And it's your fault."

"Tiger Martin!" exclaimed Einstein. "The eighth-grade terror! The biggest kid in the school! The kid who can dunk a basketball without even jumping up! Tiger Martin, the one-man football team! I'd rather fight a real tiger than fight him."

"I know, I know," Pat said nervously. He looked as if he were about to cry. "You gotta help me. It's your fault that I'm in trouble with him."

"Would you mind explaining that?" Einstein asked cautiously. "What have I got to do with you and Tiger Martin?"

"You remember that time you helped me beat Tiger Martin in a strength contest? Well, I was just telling these eighth graders how I made a fool out of Tiger and…"

"And Tiger overheard you," Einstein said. "Very smart. That's like lighting a match to see if a gas tank is full. Well, tell me the worst. What did Tiger say? And how am I involved?"

"If you hadn't helped me beat Tiger in that strength contest, I never would have said anything. So it's your fault Tiger is angry to me."

"Great reasoning," Einstein said.

"Yeah," said Pat. "Tiger was going to beat me up right away. But I convinced him that he'd have more fun if he could beat me in another strength contest." Pat paused. "The loser has to act like the winner's slave for a whole month," he added sadly.

"Can you give me one good reason why I should help you?" Einstein asked.

Pat thought for a minute. "No," he said. "But if you help me, I'll beat up anyone in the sixth grade you want me to."

Einstein laughed. "Never mind," he said. "I'll help you, but you don't have to beat up anyone for me. Maybe if you weren't so busy looking for someone to hit or to trick, you wouldn't get into so much trouble."

"I knew you'd help me, Einstein," Pat said. "And if you like, I won't pick on anyone for a whole week," he added magnanimously.

"O.K., just tell me about the contest," Einstein said.

"It can't be like the last one," Pat said, "when there were two different tests and Tiger had to choose one. Then you tricked him into choosing the wrong test. This time Tiger says that both him and me have to do the same thing."

"If you both do the same thing, how do you expect to beat Tiger?" asked Einstein. "He's much stronger than you."

"I know," Pat admitted. "But you can think of something. I'm sure of it. Can't you? Please?"

Einstein pushed back his glasses with one finger. He was quiet for several minutes. Once he shook his head and said, "That won't work." But then a smile came to his face. "Eureka!" he said.

"Huh?" said Pat. "You reeka? What does that mean?"

"That's just what Archimedes said when he discovered the answer to a puzzle," Einstein explained. "But never mind about that. Here's what we're going to do. You have to get some light string and a heavy rock. You're going to challenge Tiger to break the string tied to the rock. After he fails, you're going to do it."

"You're crazy, Einstein," said Pat. "Any string that I can break Tiger can easily break. He could probably break an anchor chain if he tried. There's no chance I can win."

"With science on your side, you can always win," Einstein said. "Here's what we're going to do. We'll tie one end of the string to some support such as a basketball hoop. The other end of the string we'll tie to the rock. Then we'll tie another string from the rock and let it hang down. Like this." Einstein took out his notepad and drew a diagram.

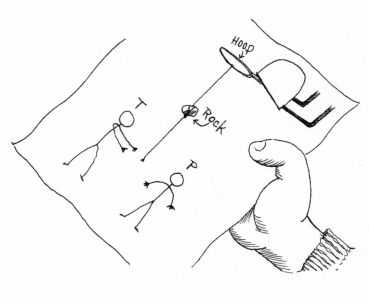

"It looks silly," objected Pat. "Tiger can easily break that string if I can."

"Tell Tiger that he has to break the *upper* string," said Einstein. "Here's what you have to do." Einstein explained rapidly to Pat.

The contest was held the next day. Many eighth graders were there to see Tiger win. Many sixth graders were there to see Pat lose.

It was no contest. No matter how hard. Tiger yanked on the bottom string, he could not break the top string. Pat, on the other hand, had no trouble in breaking the top string.

Can you solve the mystery: How did Einstein plan the contest so that Pat would win?

45

Later that day Einstein was in the school yard, explaining to some of his friends why Pat was able to break the string in the contest.

"You see," said Einstein, "which string broke depended on the way it was pulled. I told Pat to pull the bottom string slowly but steadily. The upper string broke first because it had to support the weight of the rock plus the amount of force that Pat was pulling down. The lower string just had to support the force of Pat's pull."

"But that doesn't make sense," Mike objected. "Tiger's stronger than Pat. And he was pulling harder, too. I saw him jerk down on the bottom string with a lot of strength. But he kept breaking the lower string."

"It's a matter of inertia," explained Einstein. "I knew that Tiger would be so eager to win that he'd pull down suddenly with all his strength. But the heavy rock has a lot of inertia. That is, the rock tends to remain in the same place. It takes an instant to get it moving. In that instant the force of Tiger's sudden pull broke the bottom string before the rock could start to move."

"So Tiger has to be Pat's slave for a month," said Barney. "I bet he'll love that. Pat better not push Tiger too far or Tiger will stuff Pat through the basketball hoop."

"I'm not going to worry about Pat," responded Einstein. "As soon as he won the contest, he was boasting again. It's a wonder how Pat's big head holds such a little mind."

6

The Case of the

DiRTY TRAFFiC

Do we have time for a quick cup of coffee before we leave for the town meeting?" Dr. Anderson asked his wife.

"Just about," responded Mrs. Anderson. "The meeting begins in half an hour, and I want to be on time. I'm going to write an article on the meeting for the *Tribune*. It should be a lively evening."

"Maybe Einstein can tell us how to cool the coffee more quickly," Dr. Anderson said, glancing at his older son. "Should I pour the cold milk in the coffee first and then wait five minutes before drinking it, or should I wait five minutes before adding the cold milk and then drink the coffee?"

Einstein looked up from the chocolate cake that he was devouring. "Easy, Dad," he said. "Wait five minutes before adding the cold milk. How quickly coffee cools depends upon the difference in temperature between the coffee and the air around it. If you add the cold milk right away, the difference between the temperature of the coffee and that of the air is less, so it will cool off more slowly."

"I knew you'd come up with the right answer," Dr. Anderson said affectionately. "I guess even a cup of coffee has something scientific about it."

"It sure does, Dad," responded Einstein. "Do you know that coffee is sometimes like the Earth's surface?"

"How's that, Einstein?" asked Dennis, Einstein's younger brother.

"When the coffee is ground," Einstein joked.

Dr. Anderson laughed while Mrs. Anderson and Dennis held their noses to show what they thought of the joke.

"Mom, do you know that you can clean up spilled coffee with cake?" Einstein said. "As long as it's sponge cake."

Even Dr. Anderson groaned at that. "No more, please," he said. "We'll never get to the town meeting on time."

"If you want to be on time, then it's a good idea to sit on your watch," Einstein responded. "Sorry about that."

The town meeting was in the high school auditorium. The Andersons arrived a few minutes before the meeting was scheduled to begin. Most of the seats were taken, so they had to sit toward the rear.

"Why is this meeting so crowded?" Dennis asked. "Usually we can get seats in front."

"The main item on the agenda is the new state highway," Mrs. Anderson said. "It will connect upstate with downstate and carry a lot of traffic. The town is going to decide where it will be located, east or west of Sparta."

"That should be an easy decision," Einstein observed. "If I were going to build a north-south highway, I would..."

"Sh, Einstein," said Mrs. Anderson. "The meeting is about to begin, and I have to take notes."

The meeting began. Several members of the audience stood up and presented their views. The audience seemed about equally divided: About half seemed to want the new highway to be east of town, and the other half seemed to want it west of town. Air pollution was the main issue. Most people wanted to avoid the pollution that traffic would bring if the highway was near their homes. Those who lived in the east part of town wanted the highway on the west, while the reverse was true of those who lived in the west part.

The argument had been going on for an hour when Einstein raised his hand to be recognized. The chairperson finally called on him.

"Let's hear what the young man in the back has to say," said the chairperson.

Einstein stood up. Everyone looked at him. He felt a little strange about being the center of attention of so many adults.

"Excuse me," Einstein said. "But most people will be a lot happier if you build the highway on the east of Sparta."

"How can you say that?" asked the chairperson. "The highway is to be built the same distance from town either east or west. It seems to me that half the town is going to get more air pollution than the other half no matter where we build the highway."

"That's not true," said Einstein.

Can you solve the mystery: Why did Einstein think that building the highway to the east of Sparta was better for the town?

"Would you like to explain that, young man?" asked the chairperson.

"Sure," said Einstein. "In the United States or in any other country in the temperate zone, the prevailing winds are from the west. If the highway is built west of Sparta, the winds will carry the auto exhaust and noises right to most people's homes. But if the highway is built to the east, the winds will carry the air pollutants away from Sparta."

A murmur of agreement went through the audience. "That certainly makes sense," said the chairperson. "I want to thank that young man for his contribution to this meeting. I think I'm going to call for a vote now."

As the Andersons were walking out of the auditorium after the meeting, Dennis tapped Einstein on the shoulder. "How do you know so much about cars, Einstein?" he asked.

Einstein smiled. "I like to read the life stories of cars," he said. "You know, auto-biographies."

Dr. Anderson laughed. Dennis and Mrs. Anderson held their noses.

7

The Case of the

COLD LIGHT

Einstein, I want you to come over to my house right away," Stanley said over the telephone. "This is a surefire way to use a chemical formula to make a lot of money. In fact, even if it doesn't work, I can double the money that it costs me to try it out."

"Wonderful," said Einstein. "Don't tell me. You've discovered a way to change lead into gold. Or rocks into diamonds. Or water into oil."

"Don't be silly, Einstein," Stanley declared. "I'm through with all that nonsense. It's not even my invention. I'm going to send for it through the mails. And if it doesn't work, then I'm guaranteed twice my money back."

"Oh, no," said Einstein. "Not another miracle by mail order. Haven't you been fooled enough by ads for giant ants, time machines, and green monsters? The last time you sent for something in the mail it was supposed to be unbreakable glass. It arrived in little splinters."

"I know, I know," Stanley said impatiently. "But this is different. I tell you, I can't lose. If it works, I can make millions. If it doesn't work, I still can't lose any money."

"O.K.," Einstein said cautiously. "I'll come over after I have a snack. I just came home from school, and I'm hungry."

Einstein hung up and went over to the refrigerator. A glass of milk and a slice of bread with peanut butter and jelly would be just the right thing, he decided. As Einstein ate his snack, he read from a book that he had just borrowed from the school library. The book was about science, naturally. You had to guess whether certain sayings about animals were true or false. Einstein got them all right, of course.

On the way to Stanley's house Einstein stopped to observe an ant mound, an odd-looking mushroom, which he carefully did not touch, and a circling hawk. He also picked up a rock that had an imprint of a seashell. Einstein promptly identified the rock as limestone.

By the time Einstein arrived at Stanley's house, Stanley was bursting with impatience. "How did you come here, Einstein—by the North Pole?" he asked sarcastically, pushing back his long black hair.

Einstein was imperturbable. "At least I know the difference between the North Pole and the South Pole," he said.

"What?" Stanley asked.

"The whole world," replied Einstein.

"Don't start with those silly jokes!" Stanley said. "Come upstairs to my laboratory and let me show you what I'm going to do."

The attic room that Stanley used for his "laboratory" was in its normal messy state. But one table had been cleared of its usual tangle of test tubes and chemicals. In the middle of the table was a magazine.

"Here it is," said Stanley, pointing to the magazine. "This will make me a millionaire. It can't miss."

Einstein sighed. "I'm afraid the only way you'll ever make a million dollars is by working in a mint," he said.

"Is that so," Stanley said. "Well, just read this advertisement." Stanley opened the magazine and pointed to one of the pages.

Einstein looked at the ad. It read:

MAKE YOUR OWN COLD LIGHT

This secret chemical formula, when mixed together, produces light that is 90 percent efficient. Contrast that with electric light-bulbs, which are only 4 percent efficient and give off 96 percent of their energy as waste heat. We guarantee this formula will work. If it does not work as promised, we will refund twice the money you send for the formula. This kind of light is already in use in Brazil and China. We guarantee it.

"I plan to make the chemicals in the formula and bottle them for sale," Stanley said. "They can be used as cheap sources of light. Why, you don't even need electricity. And if it doesn't work, then I get twice my money back. How can I lose?"

Einstein pushed back his glasses with one finger and thought for a minute. "The formula will work," he said. "But you will lose your money even though everything in that ad is true except that the formula is secret. Scientists have known the formula for years. You yourself have seen that cold light many times. Most people have seen it."

"Explain yourself, Einstein," Stanley said.

Can you solve the mystery: What is the cold light, and why can't Stanley use the formula to make money?

"That cold light is called luminescence," explained Einstein. "Fireflies give off that kind of light. The light is almost without heat. Half a dozen fireflies in a jar can give off enough light for you to read a book. And there are people in Brazil and China who do use fireflies for light."

"I never thought of that," Stanley said. "But does anyone know how fireflies produce their light?"

"Sure," said Einstein. "Fireflies produce light through a chemical process in their stomachs. Scientists have found that there are four chemicals involved. If you were to mix these together in a test tube, they would produce light. You can find the formulas for the chemicals in many books. They're not secret."

"But if the formula does work, then even though I paid for it, I should be able to bottle it and make money selling it to people to use for lighting," Stanley said.

"Not really," said Einstein. "The chemicals are just too expensive to use in people's homes for lighting. It would be cheaper to catch fireflies and use them. But since the formula would work, the mail-order company doesn't have to refund your money. They are only selling a readily available formula to make money for themselves."

"At least I learned something about fireflies," Stanley said sadly.

"That's something to be *bright* about," agreed Einstein. "But it's getting close to dinnertime. So as the firefly said when he started for home, 'Good-bye, I gotta *glow* now.'"

8

The Case of the

BLiND RATTLESNAKE

The exploration of the American Southwest is very interesting," Ms. Warren, Einstein's social studies teacher, said. "We've read how John Powell and his party explored the Grand Canyon by following the Colorado River and braving the rapids in four small rowboats. We've read about the Native American tribes that inhabited the Southwest for hundreds of years before Columbus. Today I'm going to read from a diary of an old gold prospector named

Rattler Pete. Can anyone guess what 'Rattler' refers to?"

Many students raised their hands. Even Pat had his hand raised. Ms. Warren looked surprised at that.

"Will you answer the question, Pat?" she asked.

"Can I leave the room, Ms. Warren?" Pat replied. "I'd like to get a drink of water."

"I should have know better than to think you were volunteering to answer a question, Pat," said Ms. Warren. "You can get a drink at the end of the period. Right now I'd like you to answer my question."

"What question was that?" Pat asked.

"A rattler!" Ms. Warren exclaimed in exasperation. "Tell the class what a rattler is."

"Huh," said Pat. "A rattle is something a baby shakes to make noise. Everybody knows that."

The class groaned.

"That's a silly answer," Ms. Warren declared. "You were just not paying attention. Will someone else tell us what a rattler is? Sally."

"Rattler is a nickname for rattlesnake," Sally said. "A baby rattle and a rattler have nothing to do with each other."

Einstein raised his hand and was recognized. "In a way, Pat is partly right," he said. "A rattlesnake got its name because of the noise it makes, a rattle. The rattle is made up of hardened loose scales that once covered the tip of the tail. A rattlesnake is very interesting because..."

"Thank you very much, Einstein, but this is not a science class," Ms. Warren said. "We're learning about history now, not rattlesnakes. I don't think the two subjects have much to do with each other."

"Science is useful in all areas," said Einstein. "I think that—"

"Not now, Einstein," Ms. Warren interrupted.

"Yeah, quiet down, Einstein," Pat said. "I want to learn some history."

"You're interested in history?" Margaret asked incredulously. "If you ever had an interest in anything besides playing tricks, it would be beginner's luck."

Ms. Warren clapped her hands firmly. "Let's stop all this nonsense," she said. "I'm going to read a passage from Rattler Pete's diary. It tells us some interesting things about gold prospecting, animals, and life in the last century on the frontier."

Ms. Warren opened a book on her desk and began to read from a page she had marked:

"Yesterday was the first day of the year 1860. When gold was discovered last year near Virginia City, Nevada, I thought I would easily strike it rich. But I've been prospecting now in these hills for weeks, and all I've found are rattlesnakes.

"I've washed out thousands of pans of likely-looking sand and gravel, hoping to see glittery particles of gold at the bottom of the pan, but no luck. Some Indians just sold me a map of a place over the mountains which is full of gold that early Spanish explorers left behind and never came back to get. A few more days here and I think I'll set out to explore. I have found some ruins that are real strange. They look as if they were built by giants. The doors are twelve feet high, and the windows in the room are eight feet above the ground. But I'm not telling anyone where they are.

"Meanwhile, I've been killing rattlesnakes all over the place. One rattlesnake I decided to keep as a pet because I got no dog and my mule died. I blinded the snake so it can't see me and bite me. It just rattles around the cabin and doesn't even know when I come near. It can't even catch the mice I try to feed it. The mice just wander around near the poor dumb snake, and it doesn't even know they're close by."

"That story is just not scientific," Einstein said, speaking out without raising his hand.

"What does science have to do with Pete's story?" Ms. Warren asked. "It's true that no one has ever found those huge ruins, but surely we can believe the rest of the story. Rattler Pete is giving us an accurate portrayal of life on the frontier in the last century."

"I know that one part of Pete's story is not true," Einstein declared. "So I just wonder if we can believe any other part of his story."

Can you solve the mystery: Which part of Rattler Pete's story did Einstein doubt?

"Just which part of Pete's story do you doubt?" Ms. Warren asked. "He never says he really found the gold that Spanish explorers supposedly left behind. And that has remained a legend. As far as his panning for gold and his experience with rattlesnakes are concerned, they certainly sound possible."

"The way Pete panned for gold is O.K.," Einstein said. "But his rattler story just shows that he never had any firsthand experience with the snakes. If he had had any, he'd have known the blinded rattler would have bitten him. Scientists have found that rattlesnakes can locate mice exactly even when they are blind. A rattlesnake has a pit on each side of its head between its eye and its nose. The pits are very sensitive heat detectors. The snake can even follow an animal's heat trail along the ground and then strike accurately when the animal comes into range. A rattlesnake can detect the warmth of a person's hand and strike at it from a few feet away."

"Pete's story was published back in 1880," Ms. Warren said. "How come Pete didn't just look up rattlesnakes in a book and find out about them? Then he could have fooled anyone."

"Because when Pete wrote the book, no one knew just how rattlesnakes stalked their prey. It wasn't until 1892 that it was noticed that a rattlesnake was attracted to a lighted match. The first experiments with a snake's heat-sensitive pits were made in 1937, long after Pete wrote the book."

"That's very interesting," said Ms. Warren. "I'm glad you listened so closely to the story."

"I just wanted to give Rattler Pete a fair *snake*," said Einstein.

9

The Case of the

DOG'S NOSE

Margaret Michaels was determined to get Einstein to make a mistake in science. Margaret was Einstein's best friend but also his rival in science. Each of them was always trying to show who knew more about science (and also baseball). So when Margaret invited Einstein to come over on Saturday to see "a very curious thing" that she had found, Einstein suspected that she had some trick in store for him.

"I just want to tell you, Margaret,"

Einstein said when he arrived on Saturday, "that I'm prepared to see through any scientific plot you've cooked up to fool me."

"Who, me?" Margaret asked innocently. "Why are you so suspicious, Einstein? Could it be that you don't know everything about science?"

"No one knows everything about science," Einstein said. "But remember, there's no such thing as the perfect crime. Even the smartest people leave clues that can trip them up. Before you teach a dog new tricks, you have to know more than the dog."

"We'll see about that," Margaret said, smiling. "But talking about dogs, it was Nova who really found what I'm going to show you." Nova was Margaret's pet dog, a springer spaniel.

"Don't tell me," said Einstein. "Nova found an old dinosaur bone in your backyard, and you want me to tell you that it's real."

"Are you finished?" Margaret asked with great dignity. "For your information, Nova did not find a dinosaur bone. And if you will just stop talking so much, I'll take you to see what Nova found."

"Sure," Einstein agreed amicably. "Say, did you hear about the dog that ate garlic so that its bark would *really* be worse that its bite?"

"Ohhh," Margaret groaned. "Don't tell me it's joke time!"

"Sorry." Einstein laughed. "Show me your 'very curious' discovery."

"Fine," said Margaret. "It's about a twenty-minute walk. Let's take Nova along. I have to walk her anyway."

Margaret lived in a house out of town. There were many forested lands around that had never been farmed because of the rocky soil in the area. After walking down the road for a while, Margaret pointed to a rarely used footpath that led up a wooded hillside.

"It's up that way," she said. "Remember I was telling you that I had seen a bright light and heard an explosion one night. Well, I thought that the sound came from this direction, but I couldn't tell exactly where.

"So four or five days after I heard the explosion, I decided to see if I could find any-

thing around. I decided to take Nova along,
because she has such a keen sense of smell.
Springer spaniels have good noses; they are
not pointers, but they're often used to track
game birds. Look at her now."

Nova was running back and forth in the woods and sniffing everything that she came across. She seemed to be having a wonderful time but hardly looked as if she were following a trail.

"If you didn't just tell me what a great tracker Nova is," said Einstein, "I'd think she was running around in circles."

Margaret laughed. "Well, she's not really tracking anything now. But last time I found some material caught on a bush, and I gave it to Nova to smell. I guess she finally got the idea. Anyway, she began to run in the woods, and I followed her. I'll show you what she found. It's just up ahead."

"Where's the material you found?" Einstein asked.

"I was so scared that I must have dropped it," Margaret said. She suddenly stopped walking. "There it is," she said, pointing to an open spot in the woods.

"What?" asked Einstein. "I can't see anything."

"Look over there." Margaret pointed to

a scorched spot on the ground and to three hollowed-out places where something heavy had pressed down. "These remind me of the prints the landing pads of a rocket would make. And that scorched place in the middle is just where a rocket flame would be."

"Oh, come on, Margaret," Einstein said. "Are you trying to tell me that E.T. just decided to come down here to visit?"

"I just don't know, Einstein," Margaret said. "Do you? It looks like a rocket took off from here. And why would anyone launch a rocket from this spot? Here's the evidence that there was something going on in this spot. I think it might have been a visitor to Earth. Can you come up with a better idea?"

Einstein looked carefully at the scorched ground and at the prints of the "landing pads." Then he pushed back his glasses and thought for a moment.

"Nova isn't the only one with a good nose," he said. "My nose is pretty good, too.

And it smells something fishy about your story."

Can you solve the mystery: How did Margaret give herself away?

Margaret laughed. "I don't see what your nose has to do with this, but I doubt your sense of smell is as good as Nova's."

"That's absolutely true," said Einstein. "A dog's sense of smell is probably a million times better than a person's. After all, a bloodhound has been known to follow a trail perfectly forty-eight hours after it was made."

"Nova is an excellent tracker," said Margaret.

"But not that good," said Einstein. "No dog is. You said you had heard an explosion and seen the flash of light four or five days before you came up here with Nova. But a scent trail is gone after three days. So Nova couldn't have led you to this spot. You just made up the story to fool me into believing that Nova had led you here. As far as the marks on the ground and the scorched grass are concerned, anyone could fake those easily."

"It wasn't so easy to make those landing-pad marks," said Margaret. "And after all that trouble, Nova's nose had to trip me up!"

"You told me that springer spaniels are not pointers," Einstein said. "In fact, as far as your story is concerned, you can say that Nova is a *dis*appointer."

10

The Case of the

HUCK FINN RAFT RACE

The first Tuesday in June was Field Day for the students at Sparta Middle School. Buses came early in the morning to take everyone up to Big Lake State Park. There would be a barbecue and picnic lunch and games all day long. There would be three-legged races, potato-bag races, and all kinds of silly competitions for the sixth, seventh, and eighth grades.

But the highlight of the day was always a special contest between the grades. Each year it was different. This year it was to be a raft race. Each grade would build its own raft. In honor of Mark Twain's story of a boy rafting down the Mississippi River, the contest was named the Huck Finn Raft Race.

Of course, the raft race was not going to take place on the Mississippi. The rafts were going to float down the river that flowed into Big Lake from the mountains up north. The river was wide enough for only three rafts for about a mile above Big Lake, so the race was about a mile long.

The rafts were to be built at the spot where the river widened. All the children would work on building their grade's raft, but only two children would go on the raft and float down the river. Wooden boards and rope were provided as building materials for the rafts.

Einstein and Margaret had been elected co-chairpersons for the sixth grade. Margaret was good at getting everyone to work on a project, even Pat and Herman. And Einstein was good at thinking of ways to use science to help do things.

"I hope you have some ideas for the race," Margaret said to Einstein when the buses arrived at Big Lake. "I can't imagine that science pays much attention to making a fast raft."

"That's true," Einstein admitted. "I don't think that rafts have come in for an awful lot of attention recently. Scientists are working on some more modern means of transportation. You can hardly blame them. There aren't many people who raft to work or school these days."

"I hope you're not saying you can't think of any way we can make the sixth grade win," Margaret said. "We were elected to make the sixth grade win, and that's what we're going to do."

"Say, did you hear about the chicken who started a race from scratch?" asked Einstein.

Margaret did not laugh.

"I guess that joke really laid an egg," Einstein said.

Margaret groaned. "Are you going to keep telling silly jokes, or are you going to come up with a way we can build a better raft?"

"How can you build a better raft?" asked Einstein. "The rafts have to be the same size, and they're all going to be built out of the same materials."

82

"Then they all should float down the river at the same speed," said Margaret. "You mean to tell me the race is going to be a three-way tie?"

"I didn't say that," said Einstein. "I have a few ideas that will help make the sixth-grade raft go faster than the others."

All morning long each grade worked on building its raft. The race was held just before lunch. Einstein chose the two sixth graders who would pilot the raft downstream. He chose Pat and Herman. Then he took them aside and whispered instructions to them. Einstein also instructed Margaret to put something else on the raft.

"I hope you know what you're doing," said Margaret. "It seems to me that's just going to make the raft go slower. And why did you pick Pat and Herman to go on the raft? They're the biggest and dumbest kids in the sixth grade."

Can you solve the mystery: What were Einstein's ideas about winning the raft race?

At the start of the race the rafts floated slowly down the river. At first they were about even. The eighth-grade raft was on one side of the river, the seventh-grade raft on the other side, and the sixth-grade raft in the middle. Slowly the sixth-grade raft began to pull ahead. By the time the rafts arrived at the finish

line, the sixth-grade raft was yards ahead.

The sixth graders yelled and cheered. The other grades booed. Pat and Herman jumped up and down on the raft, yelling, "We won, we won!" After two jumps Herman was in the water. Luckily, everyone was wearing life vests, so Herman was easily rescued.

Later Einstein, Margaret, Pat, and Herman were sitting on the ground, enjoying the barbecue lunch. Pat and Herman were so proud that Einstein had selected them for going on the raft that they had not played any tricks or picked on anyone all day long.

Some eighth graders came over to where they were eating. "All right, Einstein," said one of the eighth graders. "Tell us how you won the raft race."

"He won by picking us," said Pat. "Einstein knew Herman and I could beat you guys."

"Pat and Herman did help," said Einstein. "You see, they are the heaviest kids in the sixth grade, so I chose them. I even made Margaret load the raft with rocks so it would sink lower in the water."

"Was that what made the sixth-grade raft go faster?" asked the eighth grader.

"There were two things that helped our raft go faster," said Einstein. "First, I wanted the raft to be heavier so it would be lower in the water, and second, I told Pat and Herman to try to keep the raft in the center of the river."

"What difference did that make?" asked the eighth grader.

"The water in the middle of a river flows faster than the water at the edges of a river," explained Einstein. "Also, the fastest-flowing water is not at the surface but a short distance below the surface. That means that a raft that's deeper in the water and in the center of the river will be pushed by the fastest currents.

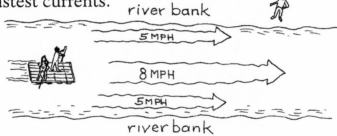

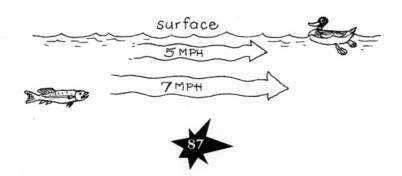

"The reason is that there's a special kind of friction in liquids called viscosity. The banks of a river slow down the water flowing nearest to them. The water in the center is farthest away from the banks so it flows fastest. In the same way, air slows down the water flowing right at the surface."

The eighth grader shook his head. "The things that science teaches you about rivers are really amazing."

"For sure," said Einstein. "A river is even a handy place for getting money."

"How's that?" asked the eighth grader.

"Because there's a bank on either side," Einstein said.